W9-ATY-592

WB 5.95

The Tip At The
End Of The Street

WB 5.95

The Tip At The End Of The Street

TOHBY RIDDLE

For everyone
at ST STEPHEN'S!

with my
best
wishes,

Tohby
Riddle

📚 Angus&Robertson
An imprint of HarperCollins*Publishers*

TO MY GOOD FRIENDS AND FAVOURITE MUSICIANS

Angus&Robertson
An imprint of HarperCollins*Publishers*, Australia

First published in Australia in 1996

Copyright © Tohby Riddle 1996

This book is copyright.
Apart from any fair dealing for the purposes of private study, research, criticism or review,
as permitted under the Copyright Act, no part may be reproduced by any process without written permission.
Inquiries should be addressed to the publishers.

HarperCollins*Publishers*
25 Ryde Road, Pymble, Sydney, NSW 2073, Australia
31 View Road, Glenfield, Auckland 10, New Zealand
77–85 Fulham Palace Road, London W68JB, United Kingdom
Hazelton Lanes, 55 Avenue Road, Suite 2900, Toronto, Ontario M5R 3L2
and 1995 Markham Road, Scarborough, Ontario M1B 5M8, Canada
10 East 53rd Street, New York NY 10032, USA

National Library of Australia Cataloguing-in-Publication data:

Riddle, Tohby.
The tip at the end of the street.

ISBN 0 207 18955 2.

I. Title.
A823.3

Printed in Hong Kong

9 8 7 6 5 4 3 2 1
99 98 97 96

ST STEPHEN'S SCHOOL
CARRAMAR
LIBRARY

'The tip! Why do you want to go there?
It's all just piles of other peoples' refuse.'

Carl and Minnie were always being told
this by their parents, but it didn't stop them.
Besides, they didn't know what 'refuse' was.

The tip was down the end of their street,
and although it smelt funny, Carl and Minnie loved it.

It was amazing what people threw away ...

'Now where on earth did you get that bicycle?'
'At the tip ...!'

'Now where on earth did you get that harpsichord?'
'At the tip ...!'

'What are you doing up there? And where on earth
did you get that flying machine?'

'Wait, don't tell me ...'

Carl and Minnie were always finding things at the tip.
Things that people didn't want any more: old books,
old chairs, old musical instruments.

One day they found an old man ...

'Now where on earth did you find that old man?'
'At the tip …!'

They asked if they could keep him.
'We can't afford to keep an old man.'

They asked again.

'And who's going to feed him?'

They asked again.

'And where are you going to keep him?'
'What about the train carriage,' they said in unison.
'What train carriage???'
'The one in the backyard.'
They pointed to it through the kitchen window.
'Now where on earth did you get that?'
'At the tip!'

Mum felt a headache coming on.
They asked again.
'Oh, okay.'

With the help of the old man, Carl and Minnie began making the train carriage into a home.

They had lots of things to make it nice — paintings,
a globe, even an old gramophone with a big brass horn,
and lots of old records to play on it.

They found everything at the tip.

The old man still needed a few more things;
a pipe, a banjo and a hat.
Carl and Minnie picked some up at the tip.

Now the old man was happy.

With his kerosene lamp burning into the early hours
of the morning, the old man could be seen reading books,
perusing the globe or listening to old records.

ST STEPHEN'S SCHOOL
CARRAMAR
LIBRARY

Carl and Minnie loved to visit the old man and he loved visitors.
He would tell them stories about another world —
one that he knew a lot about.
He called it the past and it came to life in his stories —
     giant airships ...
          terrible wars ...
               silent movie stars ...
                    and so many summers.

Sometimes the old man would reach for his banjo and play a song.
His songs were rarely the high point of Carl and Minnie's visits —
he had a rusty old voice and his banjo was never quite in tune.

But he played with great gusto, passion and conviction.
She'll be coming round the mountain when she comes,
She'll be coming round the mountain when she comes ...

If Carl or Minnie had a problem or felt sad, they knew they could
always visit the old man in his carriage and be cheered up.
He would write them a silly poem, make a toy
out of rubber bands and other bits and pieces,
or perform a magic trick.

Before they knew it they had forgotten what their problems were.

The old man ate very little but Carl and Minnie
loved to make all kinds of cakes and take them
down to his carriage.

The old man would look at their cakes and say that they were
'very adventurous and innovative chefs' — which they took
as a compliment.
'How novel to combine chocolate and sardines,'
he would say.

Then they would have a tea party which would
only be interrupted by the old man having
to wind up the gramophone.
Carl and Minnie had never heard anything like
those old records. 78s he called them.
The old man said the music was 'Ragtime' and 'Dixieland'
and songs from 'Tin-pan Alley'.
Carl and Minnie used to wonder what time Ragtime was,
and whether Tin-pan Alley was in Dixieland.

The old man was never short of an answer.

He even taught them some dances.
Carl and Minnie soon became the only kids on the block who
could do the Foxtrot.

On one of their visits a fierce storm arose and Carl and Minnie couldn't get back to the house without getting soaking wet.

The old man said not to worry because storms always pass and told them a wonderful story about a storm he had once been in — a sandstorm in the Sahara Desert.

By the soft, warm light of the old man's lamp, Carl and Minnie listened intently to the old man's story while he cooked up cups of hot cocoa and passed them around.
They asked him to do his camel impersonation at least five times.

When the storm had passed
and the stars had come out,
they stepped sleepily
back to the house
and lay down in
their moonlit beds.

As they fell asleep they
could hear the old man's
gramophone,
distant and faint,
ushering them gently
into the world of dreams.

One day Carl and Minnie went to visit the old man.
They felt like a story, like the one about his days in a city
called Shanghai; or when he'd sailed around Cape Horn in a
tall ship; or when he'd outwitted an otter in Africa;
or their favourite — the one where someone stole his
beard in a Moroccan marketplace.

Hearing the familiar sound of his gramophone,
they knocked on his carriage door using the big
brass lion door knocker they'd found at the tip.
They always tapped five times so he would know
it was them.

There was no answer.
They waited a while.

Then they knocked again. A little louder.

Still no answer.
Carl lifted Minnie up so she could look in a window.
With one hand shielding her eyes from the sun she peered
into the carriage.

The old man wasn't at his stove cooking up a hot cocoa ...
He wasn't at his bookshelf looking up a poem ...
He wasn't quietly strumming his banjo ...

He was sitting in his favourite chair.
His eyes were closed and there was a
faint smile on his face — like on the face
of the little statue they'd found at the tip —
the one he'd told them came from
India or Tibet.
His weathered hands rested on a
map of the world.

Minnie knocked against the window pane.
It didn't wake him.
She knocked again, louder and louder.
'Careful Minnie, you'll break the window.'
'But he can't hear me.'

She called out to him over and over,
but he didn't stir.
He just sat there in his chair,
in the deepest sleep.
A 78 was spinning on the gramophone.
It crackled away ...
I'm looking over
a four-leaf clover ...
... then went silent.

The old man never woke.

Sometimes Carl and Minnie go and sit in the
old train carriage and play those old records —
those 78s — on the wind-up gramophone.
If it's night time they light the lamp,
and by its soft glow, recall those stories about
ships, deserts and far away cities.

Minnie sometimes plays the banjo — the old man
taught her everything he knew — and Carl
makes very good cups of hot cocoa. They're almost
as good as his camel impersonations.

And although their parents are forever telling them
not to go there, Carl and Minnie still sometimes
visit the tip at the end of their street.

They are always surprised at what people throw away.